For Andrea and Jude ~ CR

Library of Congress Catalog Card Number : 2007032366

Original edition published in English by Little Tiger Press,

an imprint of Magi Publications, London, England, 2008.

Printed in China

Library of Congress Cataloging-in-Publication Data

Rayner, Catherine.

Harris finds his feet / Catherine Rayner.

p. cm.

Summary: Harris, a very small hare with very big feet, has an elderly Grandad who teaches him the many uses of big, strong feet and other important life lessons.

ISBN 978-1-56148-616-8 (hardcover)

[1. Hares--Fiction. 2. Foot--Fiction. 3. Grandfathers--Fiction. 4. Old age--Fiction.] I. Title.

PZ7.R2297Har 2008

[E]--dc22

2007032366

HARRIS
FINDS
HIS FEET

CATHERINE RAYNER

Intercourse, PA 17534
800/762-7171
www.GoodBooks.com

Harris was a very small
hare with very big feet.

"Why do I have such enormous feet,
 Grandad?" Harris sighed.

"All hares have big feet,
 young Harris," said Grandad
 with a whiskery smile.
"I'll show you why."

Grandad hopped high into the sky.

Harris copied.
His small, clumsy bounces
grew bigger . . .

and better . . .

and higher . . .

until he could spring,
like Grandad, into the air.

Then Grandad took
Harris up, up, up to the
very tops of the mountains.

"With your strong feet," he said,
"you can hop to the top of the world . . ."

" . . . and look out whe

he birds fly, as the wind tickles your whiskers."

Grandad showed Harris all the best things.
Like how to dig a cool resting place in the
earth when the days were hot.

They stretched out together, through long, lazy afternoons, listening to the insects buzzing an

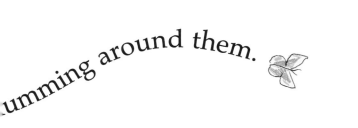umming around them.

"Look, Grandad!" Harris said. "My feet can shade me from the sun!"

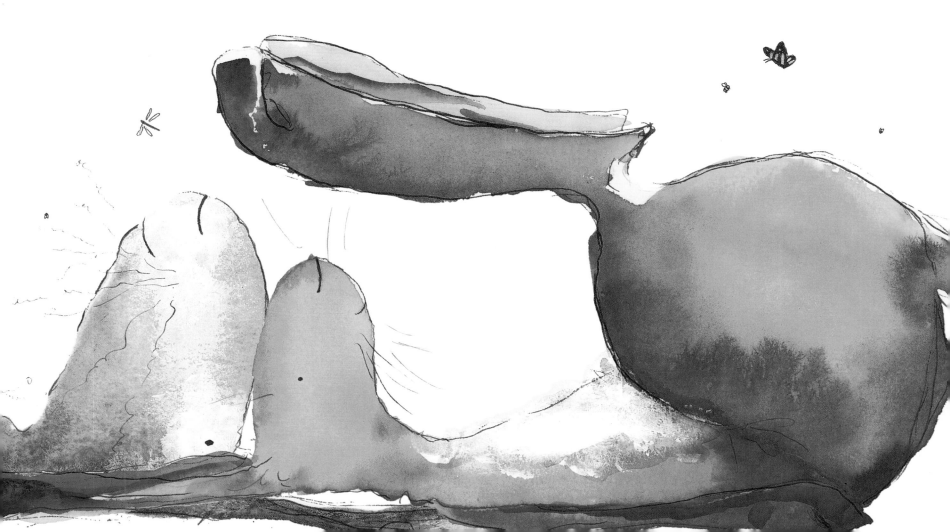

Every day Harris learned more about his world.

When a wolf came near,
Grandad sat still as a stone.
"The most important thing about your
big feet," he whispered, "is they
help you to run—

very fast."

So Harris ran, feeling the bounce in his feet
and the stretch in his legs.

He ran faster and faster . . .

as fast as fast . . .

until . . .

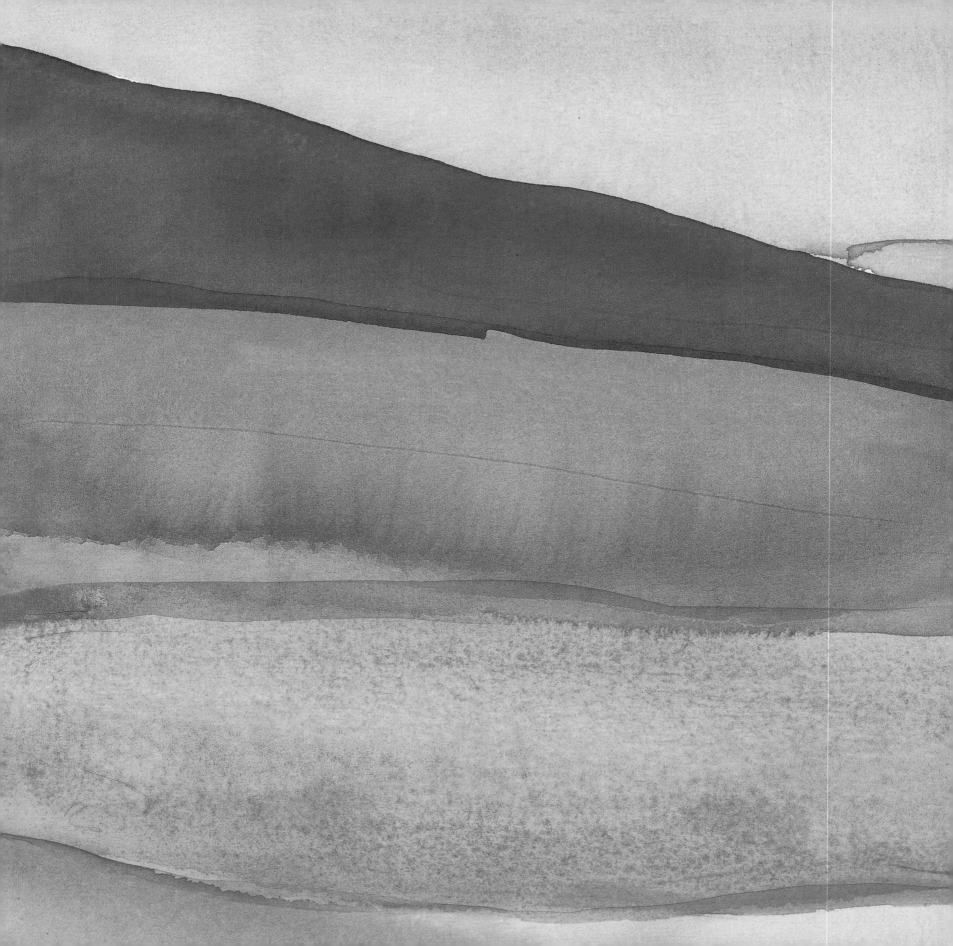

. . . he was on his own.

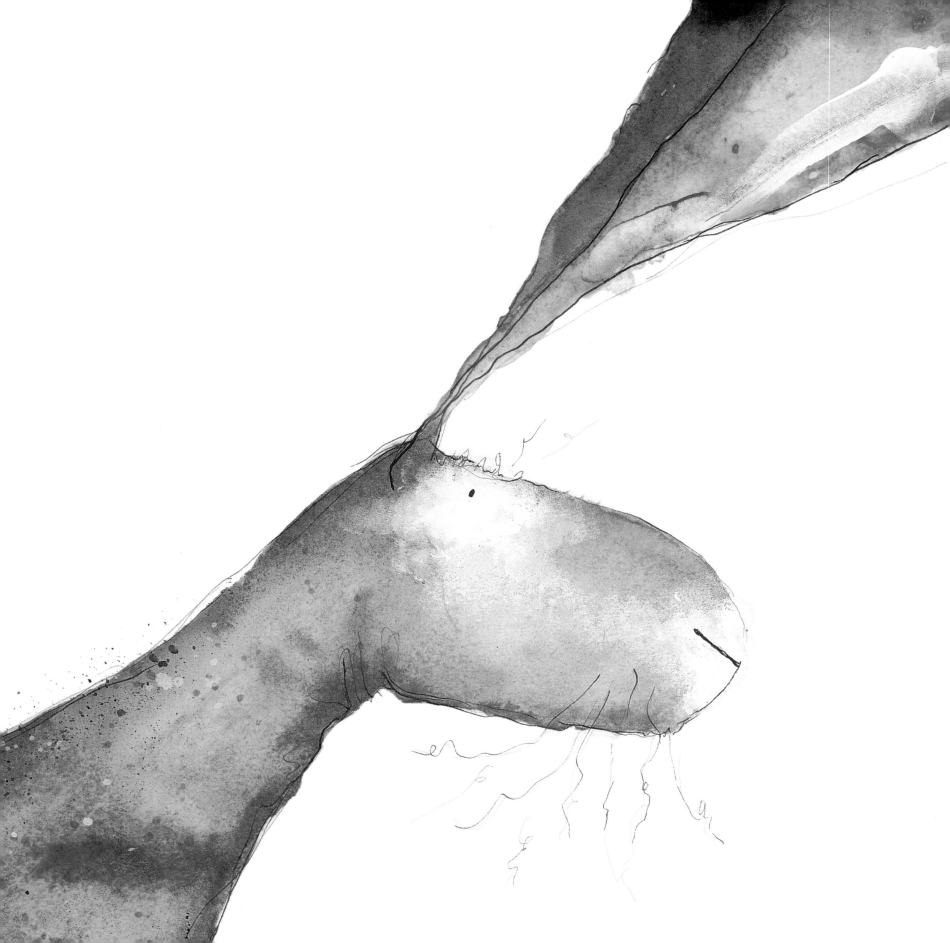

"Grandad!" Harris called, hopping back. "Why aren't you running with me?"

"Because I'm growing old, little Harris. It's your turn to run. The world is yours to explore."

And Harris ran,
   leaping over streams
   and bouncing through meadows
on his big, strong feet that would take him
                    to the end of the world—

                    and back home again.